For Ros, who introduced me to Bear,
and for Sheila – J.E.

For Ella and Anya – T.M.

Text copyright © 2005 by Jane Eagland. Illustrations © 2005 by Terry Milne.
The rights of Jane Eagland and Terry Milne to be identified as the author and illustrator of this work
have been asserted by them in accordance with the Copyright, Designs and Patents Act, 1988.
First published in Great Britain in 2005 by Andersen Press Ltd., 20 Vauxhall Bridge Road,
London SW1V 2SA. Published in Australia by Random House Australia Pty.,
20 Alfred Street, Milsons Point, Sydney, NSW 2061. All rights reserved.
Colour separated in Italy by Fotoriproduzioni Grafiche, Verona.
Printed and bound in Italy by Grafiche AZ, Verona.

10   9   8   7   6   5   4   3   2   1

British Library Cataloguing in Publication Data available.

ISBN 1 84270 363 3

This book has been printed on acid-free paper

SECOND BEST

Written by Jane Eagland

Illustrated by Terry Milne

Andersen Press
London

Bear was lonely.
He had been lying on Ellie's bed all day.
Before she left, she had put him facing Dog –
"So you will have someone to talk to," she said.
But Dog was boring.
All he thought about and all he talked about were bones.
Bear wanted Ellie to come home.
Ever since she had gone to the place called School
the days were very long.

When Ellie came home, she always told Bear what she had been doing. "We did art today," she said. "Splishy splashy colours on big pieces of paper. But Philip Thompson painted Samina's nose. Mrs Pearson told him off."

Another day she said, "We did music today. I was the wind –
whish-whish – on a cymbal. Philip Thompson was the thunder.
But his thunder was too loud. Mrs Pearson made him stop.
She said she couldn't hear the other weather at all."
Bear wished he could go to school.
It sounded fun.

Then one day Ellie came home and said, "Guess what! Tomorrow we can take our favourite toy to school." Bear felt a whoosh of excitement. At last he would go to school. At last he would meet Mrs Pearson and Samina and all the other children.
He couldn't wait.

He wasn't sure about Philip Thompson though.

In the morning Ellie usually said, "Goodbye, Bear. Goodbye, Dog," before she went to school.
"Not today," thought Bear. "I'll say, 'Goodbye, Dog,' today."
But when Ellie came into the room, she picked up Dog!

"Goodbye, Bear," she said. Then she raced downstairs.

The front door slammed.

Bear couldn't believe it. He was Ellie's favourite toy. Wasn't he?
Sadness settled in him like a stone.

All day Bear waited on Ellie's bed.
The sadness inside him grew heavier.
And it was lonely without Dog.

After a long, long time, he heard the front
door open. He heard Ellie run upstairs.

"Hello, Bear," she said.
She put Dog back on his shelf above the bed.

"It was such fun today," she said. "Everyone liked Dog.
They all wanted to pat him. But I didn't let Philip Thompson
touch him. I think he would have frightened Dog."

"I wouldn't have been frightened," thought Bear.
Then Ellie ran downstairs for her tea, and Dog started to tell
Bear about his day.

"All the children sat in a circle. Ellie held me up and told them
how she found me wrapped up under the Christmas tree."
Bear knew that. He had watched Ellie open the parcel.
He had been here *first*. It wasn't fair.
He wished Dog would go back to talking about bones.

But Dog didn't. He said, "At the end, everyone had to vote
for the toy they liked best apart from their own."
"Did you win?" asked Bear anxiously.
"No, but I came second!" said Dog.

In the night, Bear woke up. Ellie had forgotten to pull her curtains and a strange, cold light was shining into the room. Bear felt cold himself. The sadness was still there, a heavy stone inside him.

He stared out of the window at the glittering pinpricks of light in the sky. Then, something strange started to happen. Each speck of light was becoming blurred, growing bigger and bigger.

Gradually Bear saw a shape forming. The longer he stared the clearer it became, until at last, there in the sky, was a Great Bear. Slowly, it turned its head and looked long and deep into Bear's eyes. It was a kind, searching look – and Bear saw that the Great Bear knew exactly how he was feeling . . .

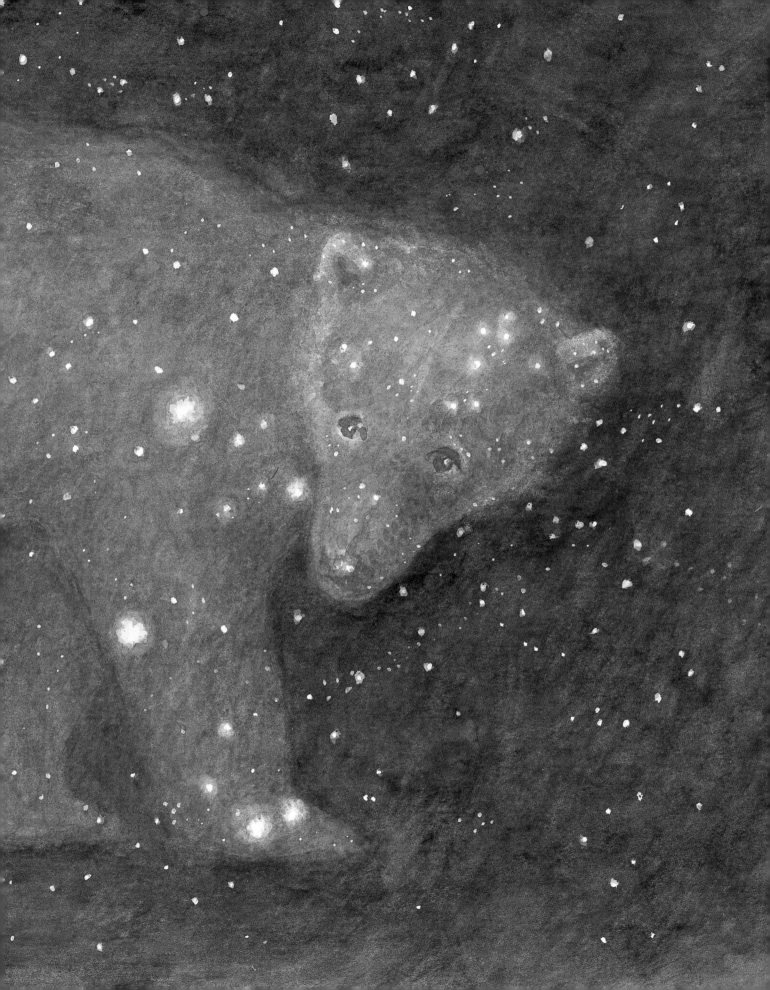

Knowing that he was understood, Bear couldn't help himself –
he gave a loud sob and Ellie woke up.

"You're crying," said Ellie. "Bear! Tell me what's wrong."

"I thought *I* was your favourite toy," said Bear. "*I* wanted to go to
school."

"Oh, Bear," said Ellie, "I'm sorry. I wanted to take you but Mum
said you were too big to go on the bus. So I took Dog instead.
I love him too. You are both my favourite toys."

The stone inside Bear disappeared.

"Next time we have a toy day I'll take you, I promise," said Ellie.
"Mum can take us in the car."
Ellie hugged Bear close and shut her eyes.
Bear looked out of the window. The Great Bear had gone.
The stars shone in the silent sky.
Bear went back to sleep.

At last the great day came. Bear went to school.
He rode in the car with Ellie and had a wonderful time.